THE GOLDEN GOOSE
and Other Favorites

drawn by L. Leslie Brooke
edited by Roberta Sewal

THE MULBERRY PRESS, INC.

The Mulberry Press, Inc.
SBN 0-88302-319-9

CONTENTS

THE GOLDEN GOOSE

THERE was once a man who had three sons, the youngest of whom was called the Simpleton. He was laughed at and despised and neglected on all occasions. Now it happened one day that the eldest son wanted to go into the forest, to hew wood, and his Mother gave him a beautiful cake and a bottle of wine to take with him, so that he might not suffer from hunger or thirst. When he came to the wood he met a little old grey man, who, bidding him good-day, said: "Give me a small piece of the cake in your wallet, and let me drink a mouthful of your wine; I am so hungry and thirsty." But the clever son answered: "If

I were to give you my cake and wine, I should have none for myself, so be off with you," and he left the little man standing there, and walked away. Hardly had he begun to hew down a tree, when his axe slipped and cut his arm, so that he had to go home at once and have the wound bound up. This was the work of the little grey man.

Thereupon the second son went into the wood, and the Mother gave him, as she had given to the eldest, a sweet cake and a bottle of wine. The little old man met him also, and begged for a small slice of cake and a drink of wine. But the second son spoke out quite plainly. "What I give to you I lose myself —be off with you," and he left the little man standing there, and walked on. Punishment was not long in coming to him, for he had given but two strokes at a tree when he cut his leg so badly that he had to be carried home.

Then said the Simpleton: "Father, let me go into the forest and hew wood." But his Father answered him: "Your brothers have done themselves much harm,

so as you understand nothing about wood-cutting you had better not try." But the Simpleton begged for so long that at last the Father said: "Well, go if you like; experience will soon make you wiser." To him the Mother gave a cake, but it was made with water and had been baked in the ashes, and with it she gave him a bottle of sour beer. When he came to the wood the little grey man met him also, and greeted him, and said: "Give me a slice of your cake and a drink from your bottle; I am so hungry and thirsty." The Simpleton replied: "I have only a cake that has been baked in the ashes, and some sour beer, but if that will satisfy you, let us sit down and eat together." So they sat themselves down, and as the Simpleton held out his food it became a rich cake, and the sour beer became good wine. So they ate and drank together, and when the meal was finished, the little man said: "As you have a good heart and give so willingly a share of your own, I will grant you good luck. Yonder stands an old tree; hew it down, and in its roots you will find something." Saying this the old man took his

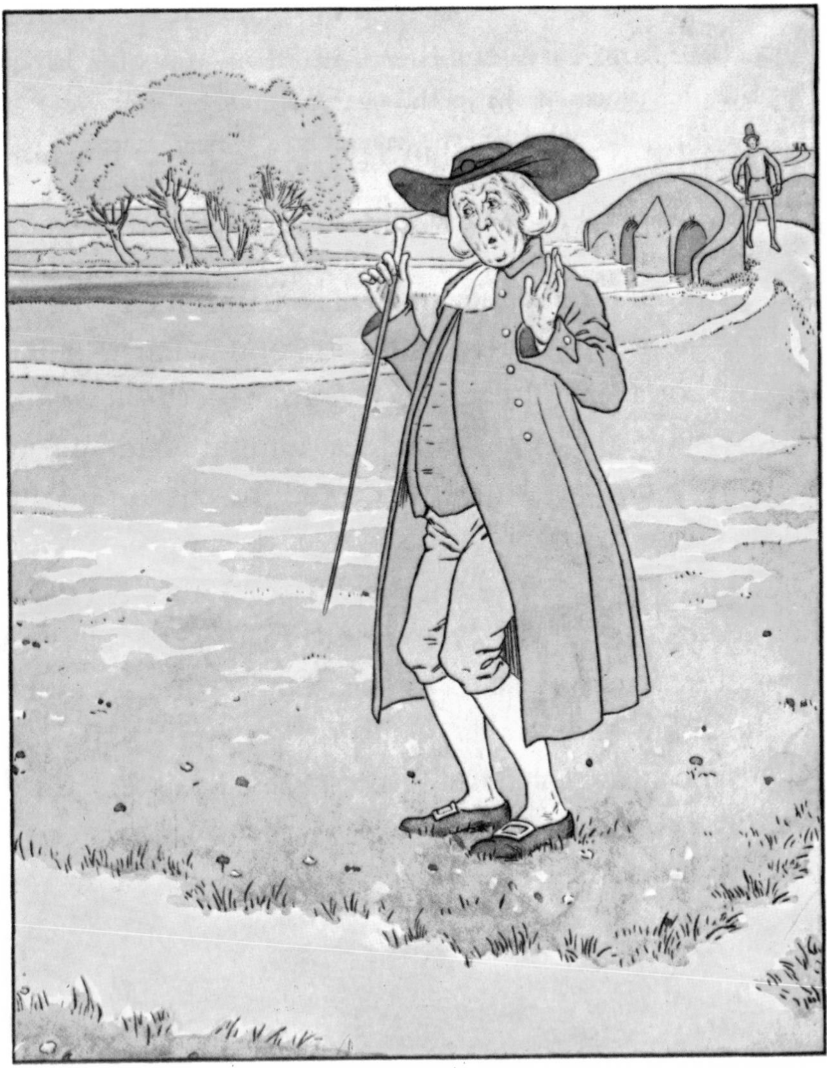

departure, and off went the Simpleton and cut down the tree. When it fell, there among its roots sat a goose, with feathers of pure gold. He lifted her out, and carried her with him to an inn where he intended to stay the night.

Now the innkeeper had three daughters, who on seeing the goose were curious to know what wonderful kind of a bird it could be, and longed to have one of its golden feathers. The eldest daughter thought to herself, "Surely a chance will come for me to pull out one of those feathers"; and so when the Simpleton had gone out, she caught the goose by the wing. But there her hand stuck fast! Shortly afterwards the second daughter came, as she too was longing for a golden feather. She had hardly touched her sister, however, when she also stuck fast. And lastly came the third daughter with the same object. At this the others cried out, "Keep off, for goodness' sake, keep off!" But she, not understanding why they told her to keep away, thought to herself, "If they go to the goose, why should not I?" She sprang forward, but as she touched her sister she too stuck fast, and pull as she might she could not get away; and thus they had all to pass the night beside the goose.

The next morning the Simpleton took the goose under his arm and went on his way, without troubling himself at all about the three girls who were hanging to the bird. There they went, always running behind him, now to the right, now to the left, whichever way he chose to go. In the middle of the fields they met the parson, and when he saw the procession he called out, "Shame on you, you naughty girls, why do you run after a young fellow in this way? Come, leave go!" With this he caught the youngest by the hand, and tried to pull her back, but when he touched her he found he could not get away, and he too must needs run behind. Then the sexton came along, and saw the parson following on the heels of the three girls. This so astonished him that he called out, "Hi! Sir Parson, whither away so fast? Do you forget that to-day we have a christening?" and ran after him, and caught him by the coat, but he too remained sticking fast.

As the five now ran on, one behind the other, two labourers who were returning from the field with their tools, came along. The parson called out to them and begged that they would set him and the sexton free. No sooner had they touched the sexton, than they too had to hang on, and now there were seven running after the Simpleton and the goose.

In this way they came to a city where a King reigned who had an only daughter, who was so serious that no one could make her laugh. Therefore he had announced that whoever should make her laugh should have her for his wife. When the Simpleton heard this he went with his goose and his train before the Princess, and when she saw the seven people all running behind each other, she began to laugh, and she laughed and laughed till it seemed as though she could never stop. Thereupon the Simpleton demanded her for his wife, but the King was not pleased at the thought of such a son-in-law, and he made all kinds of objections. He told the Simpleton that he must first bring him a man who could drink off a whole cellarful

of wine. At once the Simpleton thought of the little grey man, who would be sure to help him, so off he went into the wood, and in the place where he had cut down the tree he saw a man sitting who looked most miserable. The Simpleton asked him what was the cause of his trouble.

"I have such a thirst," the man answered, "and I cannot quench it. I cannot bear cold water. I have indeed emptied a cask of wine, but what is a drop like that to a thirsty man?"

"In that case I can help you," said the Simpleton. "Just come with me and you shall be satisfied."

He led him to the King's cellar, and the man at once sat down in front of the great cask, and drank and drank till before a day was over he had drunk the whole cellarful of wine. Then the Simpleton demanded his bride again, but the King was angry that a mean fellow everyone called a Simpleton should win his daughter, and he made new conditions. Before giving him his daughter to wife he said that the Simpleton must find a man who would eat a whole

mountain of bread. The Simpleton did not stop long to consider, but went off straight to the wood. There in the same place as before sat a man who was buckling a strap tightly around him, and looking very depressed. He said:

"I have eaten a whole ovenful of loaves, but what help is that when a man is as hungry as I am? I feel quite empty, and I must strap myself together if I am not to die of hunger."

The Simpleton was delighted on hearing this, and said: "Get up at once and come with me. I will give you enough to eat to satisfy your hunger."

He led him to the King, who meanwhile had ordered all the meal in the Kingdom to be brought together, and an immense mountain of bread baked from it. The man from the wood set to work on it, and in one day the whole mountain had disappeared.

For the third time the Simpleton demanded his bride, but yet again the King tried to put him off, and said that he must bring him a ship that would go both on land and water.

"If you are really able to sail such a ship," said he, "you shall at once have my daughter for your wife."

The Simpleton went into the wood, and there sat the little old grey man to whom he had given his cake.

"I have drunk for you, and I have eaten for you," said the little man, "and I will also give you the ship; all this I do for you because you were kind to me."

Then he gave the Simpleton a ship that went both on land and water, and when the King saw it he knew he could no longer keep back his daughter. The wedding was celebrated, and after the King's death, the Simpleton inherited the Kingdom, and lived very happily ever after with his wife.

THE STORY OF
THE THREE LITTLE PIGS

ONCE upon a time there was an old Sow with three little Pigs, and as she had not enough to keep them, she sent them out to seek their fortune.

The first that went off met a Man with a bundle of straw, and said to him, "Please, Man, give me that straw to build me a house"; which the Man did, and the little Pig built a house with it. Presently came along a Wolf, and knocked at the door, and said, "Little Pig, little Pig, let me come in."

To which the Pig answered, "No, no, by the hair of my chinny chin chin."

"Then I'll huff and I'll puff, and I'll blow your house

in!" said the Wolf. So he huffed and he puffed, and he blew his house in, and ate up the little Pig.

The second Pig met a Man with a bundle of furze, and said, "Please, Man, give me that furze to build a house"; which the Man did, and the Pig built his house.

Then along came the Wolf and said, "Little Pig, little Pig, let me come in."

"No, no, by the hair of my chinny chin chin."

"Then I'll puff and I'll huff, and I'll blow your house in!" So he huffed and he puffed, and he puffed and he huffed, and at last he blew the house down, and ate up the second little Pig.

The third little Pig met a Man with a load of bricks, and said, "Please, Man, give me those bricks to build a house with"; so the Man gave him the bricks, and he built his house with them. So the Wolf came, as he did to the other little Pigs, and said, "Little Pig, little Pig, let me come in."

"No, no, by the hair of my chinny chin chin."

"Then I'll huff and I'll puff, and I'll blow your house in."

Well, he huffed and he puffed, and he huffed and he puffed, and he puffed and he huffed; but he could *not* get the house down. When he found that he could not, with all his huffing and puffing, blow the house down, he said, "Little Pig, I know where there is a nice

field of turnips."

"Where?" said the little Pig.

"Oh, in Mr. Smith's home-field; and if you will be ready to-morrow morning, I will call for you, and we will go together and get some for dinner."

"Very well," said the little Pig, "I will be ready. What time do you mean to go?"

"Oh, at six o'clock."

Well, the little Pig got up at five, and got the turnips and was home again before six. When the Wolf came he said, "Little Pig, are you ready?"

"Ready!" said the little Pig, "I have been and come back again, and got a nice pot-full for dinner."

The Wolf felt very angry at this, but thought that he would be *up* to the little Pig somehow or other; so he said, "Little Pig, I know where there is a nice apple-tree."

"Where?" said the Pig.

"Down at Merry-garden," replied the Wolf; "and if you will not deceive me I will come for you, at five o'clock to-morrow, and we will go together and get some apples."

Well, the little Pig woke at four the next morning, and bustled up, and went off for the apples, hoping to get back before the Wolf came; but he had farther to go, and had to climb the tree, so that just as he was coming down from it, he saw the Wolf coming, which, as you may suppose, frightened him very much. When the

Wolf came up he said, "Little Pig, what! are you here before me? Are they nice apples?"

"Yes, very," said the little Pig; "I will throw you down one." And he threw it so far that, while the Wolf was gone to pick it up, the little Pig jumped down and ran home.

The next day the Wolf came again, and said to the little Pig, "Little Pig, there is a Fair in the Town this afternoon: will you go?"

"Oh, yes," said the Pig, "I will go; what time shall you be ready?"

"At three," said the Wolf.

So the little Pig went off before the time, as usual, and got to the Fair, and bought a butter churn, and was on his way home with it when he saw the Wolf coming. Then he could not tell what to do. So he got into the churn to hide, and in doing so turned it around, and it began to roll, and rolled down the hill with the Pig inside it, which frightened the Wolf so much that he ran home without going to the Fair.

He went to the little Pig's house, and told him how

frightened he had been by a great round thing which came down the hill past him.

Then the little Pig said, "Hah! I frightened you, did I? I had been to the Fair and bought a butter churn, and when I saw you I got into it, and rolled down the hill."

Then the Wolf was very angry indeed, and declared he *would* eat up the little Pig, and that he would get down the chimney after him.

When the little Pig saw what he was about, he hung on the pot full of water, and made up a blazing fire, and, just as the Wolf was coming down, took off the cover of the pot, and in fell the Wolf. And the little Pig put on the cover again in an instant, boiled him up, and ate him for supper, and lived happy ever after.

HEY! DIDDLE, DIDDLE

Hey! diddle, diddle,
The cat and the fiddle,
The cow jumped over the moon;
The little dog laughed
To see the sport,
While the dish ran away with the spoon.

HEY DIDDLE · DIDDLE

TOMMY SNOOKS AND BESSY BROOKS

As Tommy Snooks and Bessy Brooks
Were walking out one Sunday,
Says Tommy Snooks to Bessy Brooks,
"To-morrow will be Monday."

45

THERE WAS A LITTLE BOY

There was a little boy and a little girl
Lived in an alley;
Says the little boy to the little girl,
"Shall I, oh! shall I?"

Says the little girl to the little boy,
"What shall we do?"
Says the little boy to the little girl,
"I will kiss you."

AS I WAS GOING UP
PIPPEN-HILL

As I was going up Pippen-hill,
Pippen-hill was dirty,
There I met a pretty miss,
And she dropped me a curtsey.

Little miss, pretty miss,
Blessings light upon you!
If I had half-a-crown a day
I'd spend it all on you.

GOOSEY, GOOSEY, GANDER

Goosey, goosey, gander,
Where shall I wander?
Upstairs, downstairs,
And in my lady's chamber.
There I met an old man
That would not say his prayers;
I took him by the left leg,
And threw him downstairs.

I HAD A LITTLE PONY

I had a little pony,
His name was Dapple-grey;
I lent him to a lady,
To ride a mile away.
She whipped him, she slashed him,
She rode him through the mire;
I would not lend my pony now
For all the lady's hire.

WHAT ARE LITTLE BOYS MADE OF?

What are little boys made of, made of?
What are little boys made of?
"Snips and snails, and puppy-dogs' tails;
And that's what little boys are made of,
                    made of."
What are little girls made of, made of,
                    made of?
What are little girls made of?
"Sugar and spice, and all that's nice;
And that's what little girls are made of,
                    made of."

GIRLS AND BOYS, COME OUT TO PLAY

Girls and boys, come out to play;
The moon doth shine as bright as day;
Leave your supper, and leave your sleep,
And come with your playfellows into the street.
Come with a whoop, come with a call,
Come with a good will or not at all.
Up the ladder and down the wall,
A halfpenny roll will serve us all.
You find milk, and I'll find flour,
And we'll have a pudding in half-an-hour.

BARBER, BARBER

Barber, barber, shave a pig;
How many hairs will make a wig?
"Four-and-twenty, that's enough."
Give the barber a pinch of snuff.

LADYBIRD, LADYBIRD

Ladybird, ladybird, fly away home;
Thy house is on fire, thy children all gone—
All but one, and her name is Ann,
And she crept under the pudding-pan.